CHRISTMAS
STORIES AND POEMS
Illustrated by Lisa McCue

Troll Associates

For Richard
Love, Mommy

Illustrations copyright © 1994 by Lisa McCue.
Text copyright © 1994 by Troll Associates, Inc.
WhistleStop is a trademark of Troll Associates.

Printed in Mexico

10   9   8   7   6   5   4   3   2   1

Grateful acknowledgment is made to the following for permission to reprint the
stories and poems in this book. Every effort has been made to secure the necessary
permissions and make full acknowledgment for their use. If notified of any errors, the publisher
will gladly make the necessary corrections in future editions.

Norma Rose Toron for *The Mouse in the Manger* and *Christmas Cookies*,
copyright © 1994 by Norma Rose Toron. Reprinted with permission of the author.

Contents

A Christmas Wish

traditional

Sing ho! Sing hey!
For Christmas Day!
Braid mistletoe and holly,
For friendship grows
In winter snows,
And so let's all be jolly.

We Wish You a Merry Christmas
traditional

We wish you a Merry Christmas,
We wish you a Merry Christmas,
We wish you a Merry Christmas
And a Happy New Year!

Good tidings we bring,
To you and your kin,
Good tidings for Christmas
And a Happy New Year!

Baboushka

traditional

Once upon a time, in a tiny cottage deep in the forest, there lived an old woman called Baboushka. Baboushka's home was not on the road to anywhere. Baboushka never had visitors.

One day, much to her surprise, Baboushka heard a knock at her door. Quickly she opened it to see the strangest sight she'd ever seen.

Three kings stood in the darkness. Snow speckled their fine clothes, richly woven of gold and deep, bright colors. One king wore a silver crown atop his coppery curls. Another king had shining rings of ruby and emerald. The last king bore a shawl of pearls and velvet.

"Come in and warm yourself by the fire," Baboushka urged them in spite of her awe. "What brings you out on this bitter night?"

"We are searching for a baby prince," answered the king wearing the silver crown. "His star has guided us all this way, but we are weary and need to rest a bit."

"A star to lead the way to a baby prince!" Baboushka exclaimed. "What can this mean?"

Then the king explained that the star was a special sign that had been sent to lead them to the birthplace of a holy child. The three kings, for it was they, showed Baboushka the rare and precious gifts they'd brought to give the baby Jesus when they found him.

Baboushka's head was filled with wonder at the thought of all she had heard. "I wish I could see this child," she whispered.

"Come with us," the men cried. "Help us in our search."

Baboushka sighed. "I am too old to travel," she said simply.

The three kings ate and rested. When they were ready, they thanked Baboushka and set off again.

Baboushka's little house seemed terribly empty when they had gone. She sat and rocked by the fire, a thoughtful look on her face. At last she leapt to her feet. "I will!" she cried. "I will find this child and see him for myself!"

Carefully, Baboushka packed a small bundle of treasures to bring as gifts to the holy child. A carved wooden horse, a glass doll, a cloth ball, some twig figures, painted pine cones, dried berries, and pretty feathers—all went into the bundle.

Then Baboushka dressed herself warmly and set off in the direction of the three travelers. Falling snow had covered their tracks, and soon Baboushka could not be sure of the path.

Deep in the forest, trees hid the sky, and Baboushka could not see the star. By the time she reached the open meadows, dawn had lightened the sky. Baboushka began to fear she was lost.

Soon she came upon a shepherd tending his flock on a hillside.

"Please, is the little Christ child here?" she asked hopefully.

The shepherd shook his head and Baboushka sighed. Still, she traveled on, and of everyone she met she asked the same question. But none could help her.

Baboushka never gave up. She walked and walked. Sometimes she would come upon a child. Eagerly, she would look to see—could it be the child she was searching for?

And though it never was, always Baboushka would reach into her pack. Smiling, she would bring forth a tiny toy to make the child laugh.

And so Baboushka traveled on, always searching. They say that to this very day she is searching still. All day she walks, and all night she crafts small treasures to add to her pack.

And especially at Christmastime, children watch for Baboushka. For they know that if they spy her they can be sure of getting a special treasure from her wondrous pack.

A Christmas ABC
by Florence Johnson

A is for angels from Heaven above.

B is for bells, ringing news of God's love.

C is for Christmas, our most joyful day.

D is for Dancer, who pulls Santa's sleigh.

E is for evergreen, a fine Christmas tree.

F is for flower, so pretty to see.

G is for gifts for our friends big and tiny.

H is for holly with leaves green and shiny.

I is for icicles agleam in the sun.

J is for Jesus, the holiest one.

K is for kitten, a warm Christmas ball.

L is for lamp, a bright welcome to all.

M is for mailbox with mail overflowing.

N is for neighbors, their cold faces glowing.

O is for ornaments, cheery and gleaming.

P is for plum pudding, tasty and steaming.

Q is for quilt for a long winter's nap.

R is for ribbon, your presents to wrap.

S is for Santa Claus, stockings, and sleigh.

T is for tree, shining on Christmas Day.

U is for all that is under the tree.

V is for voices, singing with glee.

W is for wreath, the best one we found.

X is for kisses (and hugs) all around.

Y is for Yuletide, the time of good cheer.

Z is for *Zoom!* Santa'll be back next year.

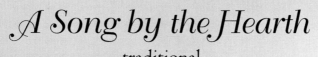

A Song by the Hearth

traditional

Sing we all merrily,
Christmas is here,
The day we love best
Of days in the year.

Bring forth the holly,
The box, and the bay.
Deck out our cottage
For glad Christmas Day.

Sing we all merrily,
Draw round the fire,
Sister and brother,
Mother and father.

The Mouse in the Manger
by Norma Rose

The manger where the baby Jesus was born was home to many animals. Most people know about the ox and the lamb, but it is not so well-known that there was also a tiny mouse. He lived in a corner under a wisp of hay, and he was good friends with the other animals.

Naturally, the mouse saw all that went on that very first Christmas. He watched the little cradle rock and heard the baby softly cooing. He looked in wonder at the shepherds as they prayed and left their simple gifts—bread and cheese for Mary and Joseph to eat or soft fluffs of lamb's wool to warm the baby. Humble townspeople came offering their music and song to honor the newborn prince.

At last Tiny Mouse blinked in astonishment as three great kings appeared. Each knelt and laid his precious gifts. There were gold and jewels and rare and wonderful spices.

Tiny Mouse sighed. "What have I to give? I must find something, I must!"

"Hush, little mouse," said the lamb. "You do not need a gift. Your love is enough."

But Tiny Mouse would not give up. He thought and thought. He crept closer and closer to the cradle. "Perhaps if I can see his face," he thought. "That might give me an idea."

A corner of blanket trailed over the cradle's edge. Bravely, Tiny Mouse tiptoed up. When he got to the top, he stopped and stared.

The beautiful baby was sleeping. Slowly, gently, the blanket rose and fell with each baby breath. Softly, quietly, the infant sighed as he dreamed. Tiny Mouse was so entranced, he forgot where he was. And so, leaning forward for a closer look, he lost his balance, and fell with a *plop!* into the cradle!

Uh-oh! The baby's eyes flew open. Tiny Mouse scrambled to get away before he was seen. But the sides of the cradle were steep. He ran and he ran, but he couldn't get anywhere.

Scritch, scritch, scritch. Tiny Mouse's feet skittered back and forth. But there was another noise, too. *Shhh, shhh, shhh.* What was that sound? Tiny Mouse grew still. Then he turned around. The baby Jesus was laughing!

"Oh, Tiny Mouse," a low voice spoke. "You have brought the best gift of all, the gift of happiness and laughter on this cold, dark night." Tiny Mouse looked up to see Mary smiling down on him.

Then Mary held out her hand. Slowly, timidly, Tiny Mouse climbed on, and Mary lifted him out and placed him on the floor.

"Thank you, little mouse, for lightening our hearts," she said.

Tiny Mouse had found a gift for the baby Jesus after all.

Christmas Cookies
by Norma Rose

Sift the flour, mix the butter,
Roll the dough for the cookie cutter.
A white sugar star, a red Christmas bell,
A brown teddy bear with a gingery smell.

Christmas cookies taste so sweet,
They're fun to bake and good to eat.

Carol

from *The Wind in the Willows*

by Kenneth Grahame

Villagers all, this frosty tide,
Let your doors swing open wide,
Though wind may follow and snow betide
Yet draw us in by your fire to bide;
Joy shall be yours in the morning!

Here we stand in the cold and the sleet,
Blowing fingers and stamping feet,
Come from far away, you to greet—
You by the fire and we in the street—
Bidding you joy in the morning!

For ere one half of the night was gone,
Sudden a star has led us on,
Raining bliss and benison—
Bliss tomorrow and more anon,
Joy for every morning!

Good man Joseph toiled through the snow—
Saw the star o'er the stable low;
Mary she might not further go—
Welcome thatch and litter below!
Joy was hers in the morning!

And then they heard the angels tell,
"Who were the first to cry Nowell?
Animals all, as it befell,
In the stable where they did dwell!
Joy shall be theirs in the morning!"

A Visit from Santa Claus

anonymous

He comes in the night! He comes in the night!
He softly, silently comes,
While the sweet little heads on the pillows so white
Are dreaming of bugles and drums.

He cuts through the snow like a ship through the foam,
While the white flakes round him whirl.
Who tells him I know not, but he finds the home
Of each good little boy and girl.

The little red stockings he silently fills,
Till the stockings will hold no more.
The bright little sleds for the great snow hills
Are quickly set down on the floor.
Then Santa Claus magically flies to the roof
And glides to his seat in the sleigh.
You can't even hear a reindeer's hoof
As they noiselessly gallop away.